W9-AVA-065

Grayslake Area Public Library District
Grayslake, Illinois

1. A fine will be charged on each book which is not returned when it is due.

2. All injuries to books beyond reasonable wear and all losses shall be made good to the satisfaction of the Librarian.

3. Each borrower is held responsible for all books drawn on his card and for all fines accruing on the same.

DEMCO

As World War II raged on, a young, scrawny Steve Rogers was selected to participate in Project: Rebirth to become the living embodiment of the American Spirit: *Captain America!*

Nearing the end of World War II, Captain America and Bucky were tasked with guarding an experimental remote-controlled drone bomber. The drone was booby-trapped, however, and in the subsequent explosion, Bucky was killed and Cap was thrown into the ocean below--where he would stay in suspended animation until he was discovered by the modern day Avengers!

Feeling out of place in the modern world, Cap reached out to his former wartime commanding officer, General Jacob Simon. Now an elderly man, Simon became a touchpoint for Cap in understanding the radical changes to the world since he had been on ice. After Simon passed away, Cap and the Avengers rushed out to face the time-traveling chrono-terrorist Kang. After seemingly defeating the Avengers, Kang banished Cap back in time to V-J Day...

CAPTAIN AMERICA:
MAN OUT OF TIME, PART 5

Mark Waid – Writer
Jorge Molina – Penciler
Karl Kesel – Inker
Frank D'Armata – Colorist
VC's Joe Sabino – Letterer & Production
Bryan Hitch, Paul Neary & Paul Mounts – Cover Art
Lauren Sankovitch – Associate Editor
Tom Brevoort – Editor
Axel Alonso – Editor in Chief
Joe Quesada – Chief Creative Officer
Dan Buckley – Publisher
Alan Fine – Executive Producer

visit us at www.abdopublishing.com

Reinforced library bound edition published in 2012 by Spotlight, ABDO Group, 8000 West 78th Street, Edina, Minnesota 55439. Spotlight produces high-quality reinforced library bound editions for schools and libraries. Published by agreement with Marvel Entertainment, LLC. The stories, characters, and incidents mentioned are entirely fictional. All rights reserved. Used under authorization.

Printed in the United States of America, Melrose Park, Illinois.
052011
092011
♲ This book contains at least 10% recycled materials.

Library of Congress Cataloging-in-Publication Data

Waid, Mark.
  Man out of time / writer, Mark Waid ; penciler, Jorge Molina.
     v. cm.
  Summary: Frozen in suspended animation for over sixty years, World War II superhero Captain America, aka Steve Rogers, wakes up in the twenty-first century and must adapt to a very changed world.
  ISBN 978-1-59961-936-1 (v. 1) -- ISBN 978-1-59961-937-8 (v. 2) -- ISBN 978-1-59961-938-5 (v. 3) -- ISBN 978-1-59961-939-2 (v. 4) -- ISBN 978-1-59961-940-8 (v. 5)
  1. Graphic novels. [1. Graphic novels. 2. Superheroes--Fiction. 3. Space and time--Fiction.] I. Molina, Jorge, 1984- ill. II. Title.
  PZ7.7.W35Man 2011
  741.5'973--dc22
                         2011013320

All Spotlight books are reinforced library bindings and manufactured in the United States of America.

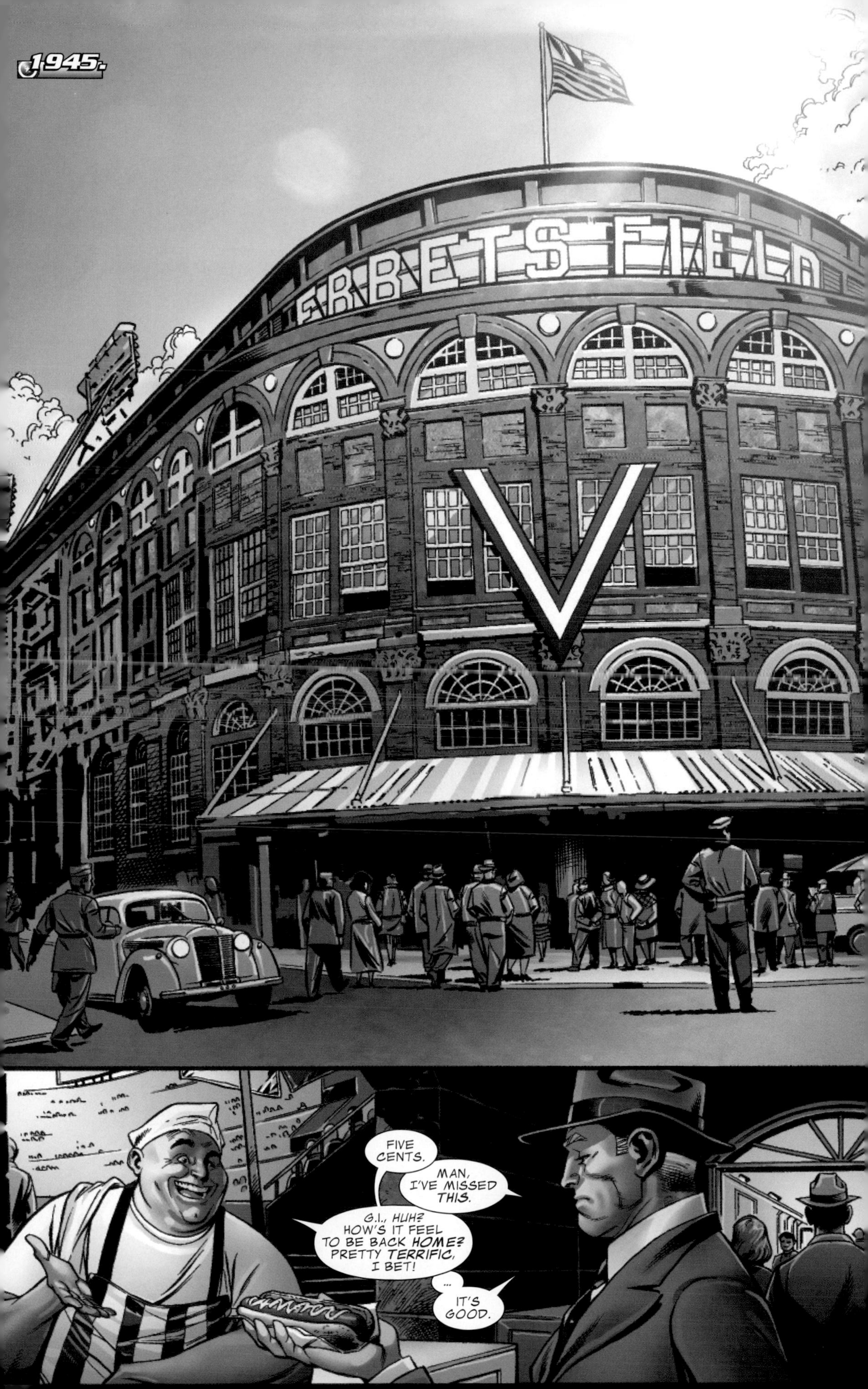
1945.
FIVE CENTS.
MAN, I'VE MISSED THIS.
G.I., HUH? HOW'S IT FEEL TO BE BACK HOME? PRETTY TERRIFIC, I BET!
... IT'S GOOD.

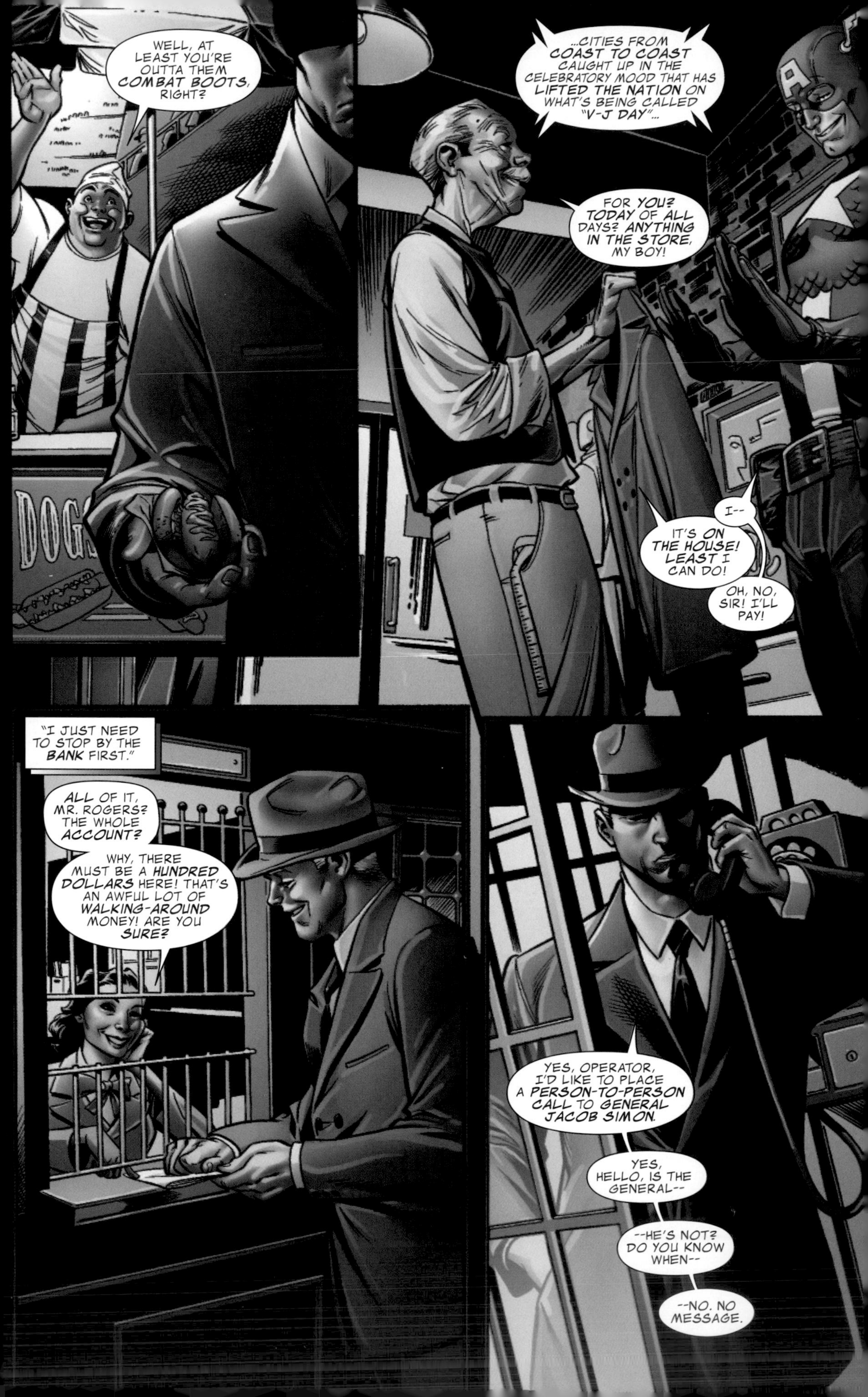
WELL, AT LEAST YOU'RE OUTTA THEM COMBAT BOOTS, RIGHT?
DOGS
...CITIES FROM COAST TO COAST CAUGHT UP IN THE CELEBRATORY MOOD THAT HAS LIFTED THE NATION ON WHAT'S BEING CALLED "V-J DAY"...
FOR YOU? TODAY OF ALL DAYS? ANYTHING IN THE STORE, MY BOY!
I--
IT'S ON THE HOUSE! LEAST I CAN DO!
OH, NO, SIR! I'LL PAY!
"I JUST NEED TO STOP BY THE BANK FIRST."
ALL OF IT, MR. ROGERS? THE WHOLE ACCOUNT?
WHY, THERE MUST BE A HUNDRED DOLLARS HERE! THAT'S AN AWFUL LOT OF WALKING-AROUND MONEY! ARE YOU SURE?
YES, OPERATOR, I'D LIKE TO PLACE A PERSON-TO-PERSON CALL TO GENERAL JACOB SIMON.
YES, HELLO, IS THE GENERAL--
--HE'S NOT? DO YOU KNOW WHEN--
--NO. NO MESSAGE.

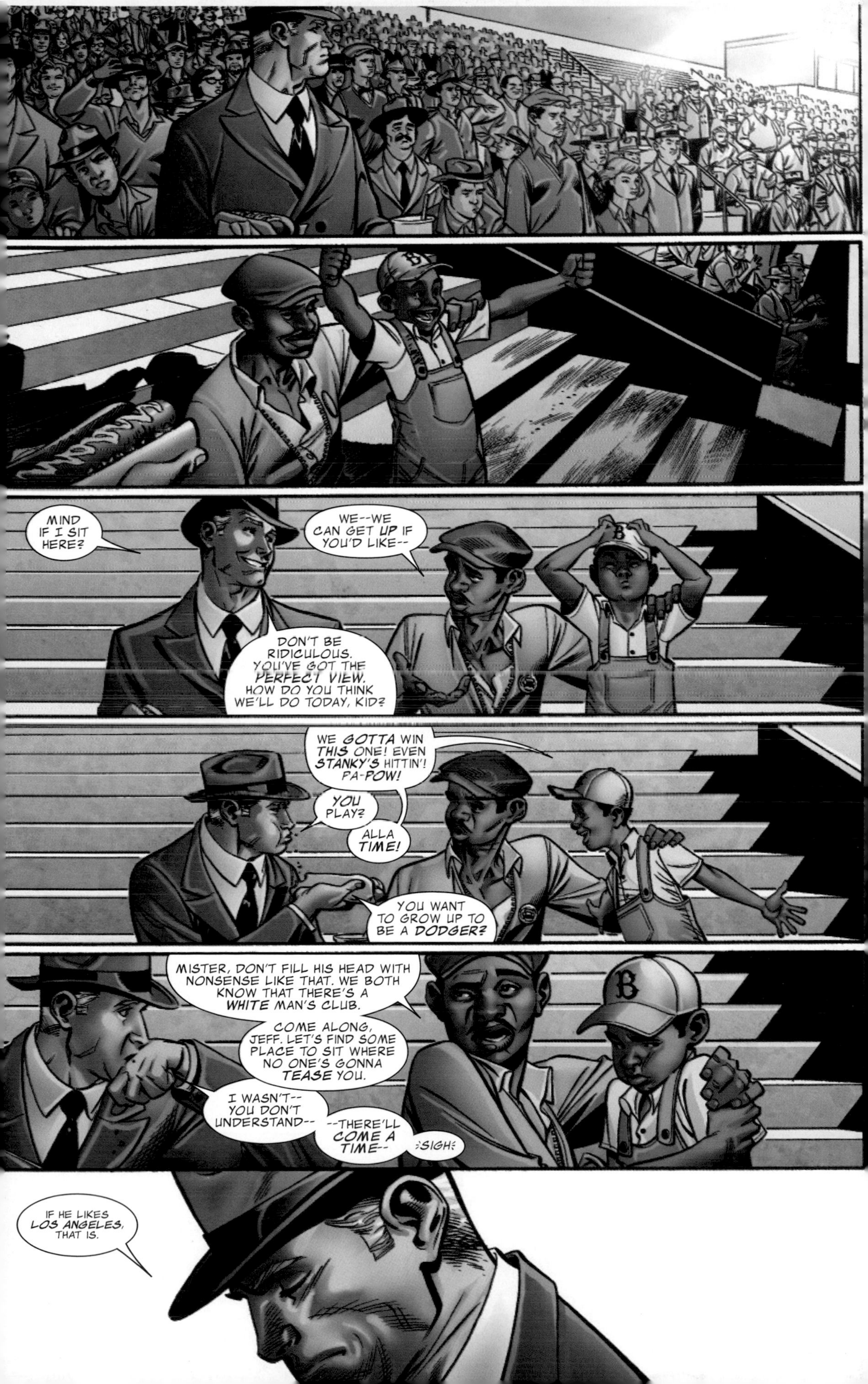
MIND IF I SIT HERE?
WE--WE CAN GET UP IF YOU'D LIKE--
DON'T BE RIDICULOUS. YOU'VE GOT THE PERFECT VIEW. HOW DO YOU THINK WE'LL DO TODAY, KID?
WE GOTTA WIN THIS ONE! EVEN STANKY'S HITTIN'! PA-POW!
YOU PLAY?
ALLA TIME!
YOU WANT TO GROW UP TO BE A DODGER?
MISTER, DON'T FILL HIS HEAD WITH NONSENSE LIKE THAT. WE BOTH KNOW THAT THERE'S A WHITE MAN'S CLUB.
COME ALONG, JEFF. LET'S FIND SOME PLACE TO SIT WHERE NO ONE'S GONNA TEASE YOU.
I WASN'T-- YOU DON'T UNDERSTAND--
--THERE'LL COME A TIME--
SIGH
IF HE LIKES LOS ANGELES, THAT IS.

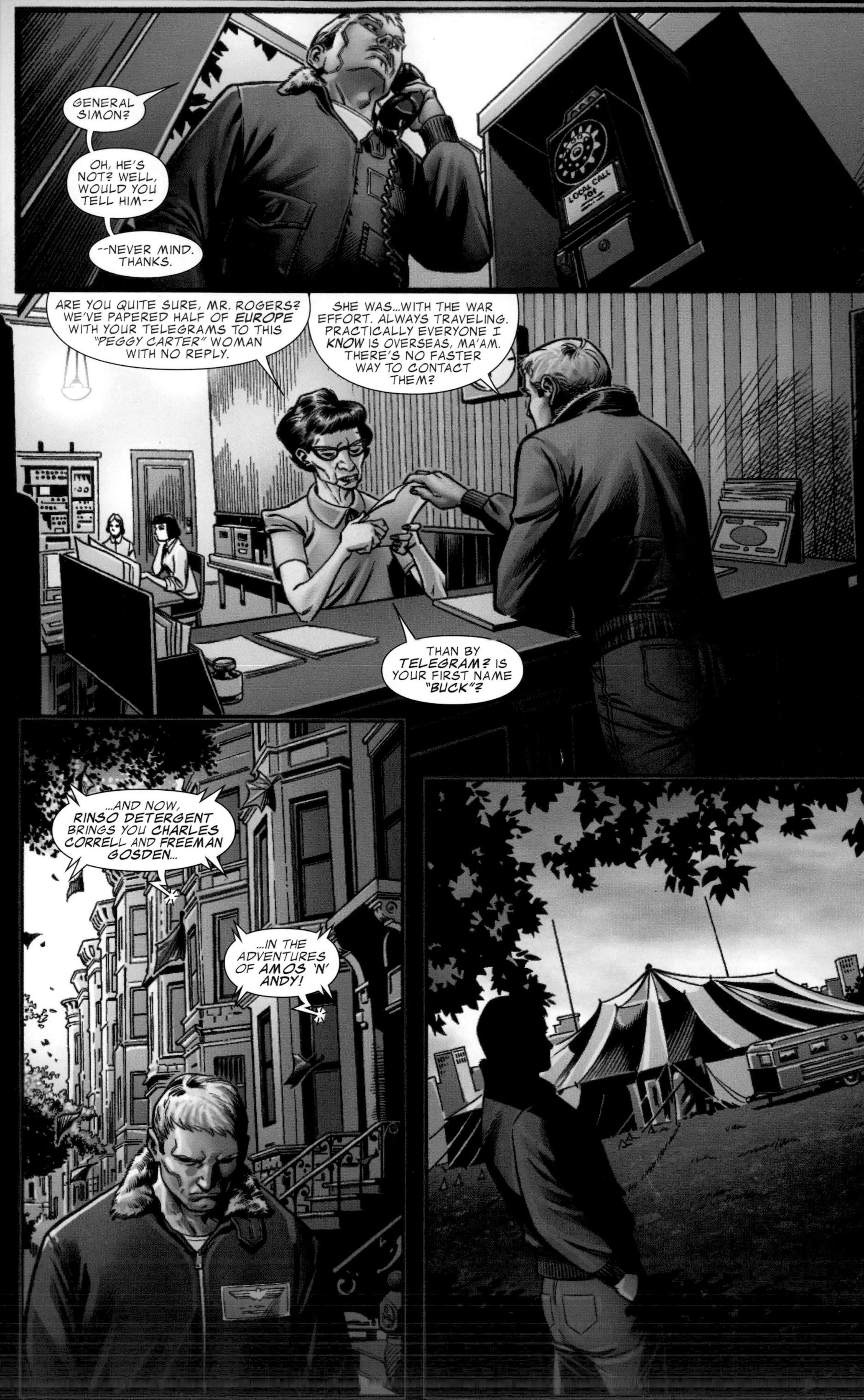
GENERAL SIMON?
OH, HE'S NOT? WELL, WOULD YOU TELL HIM--
--NEVER MIND. THANKS.
ARE YOU QUITE SURE, MR. ROGERS? WE'VE PAPERED HALF OF EUROPE WITH YOUR TELEGRAMS TO THIS "PEGGY CARTER" WOMAN WITH NO REPLY.
SHE WAS...WITH THE WAR EFFORT. ALWAYS TRAVELING. PRACTICALLY EVERYONE I KNOW IS OVERSEAS, MA'AM. THERE'S NO FASTER WAY TO CONTACT THEM?
THAN BY TELEGRAM? IS YOUR FIRST NAME "BUCK"?
...AND NOW, RINSO DETERGENT BRINGS YOU CHARLES CORRELL AND FREEMAN GOSDEN...
...IN THE ADVENTURES OF AMOS 'N' ANDY!

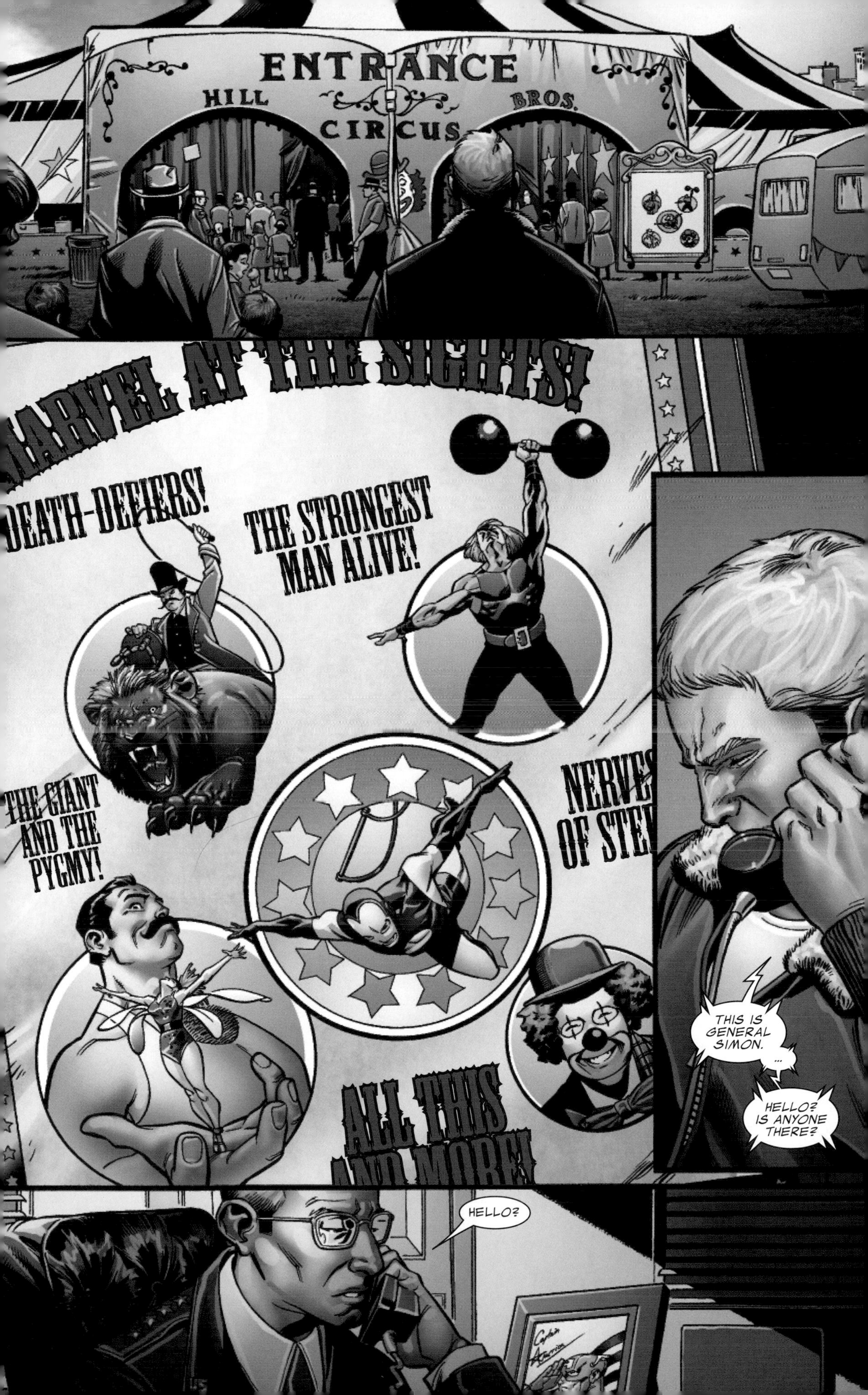

ENTRANCE
HILL BROS. CIRCUS
ARVEL AT THE SIGHTS!
DEATH-DEFIERS!
THE STRONGEST MAN ALIVE!
THE GIANT AND THE PYGMY!
NERVES OF STE
ALL THIS AND MORE!
THIS IS GENERAL SIMON.
...
HELLO? IS ANYONE THERE?
HELLO?

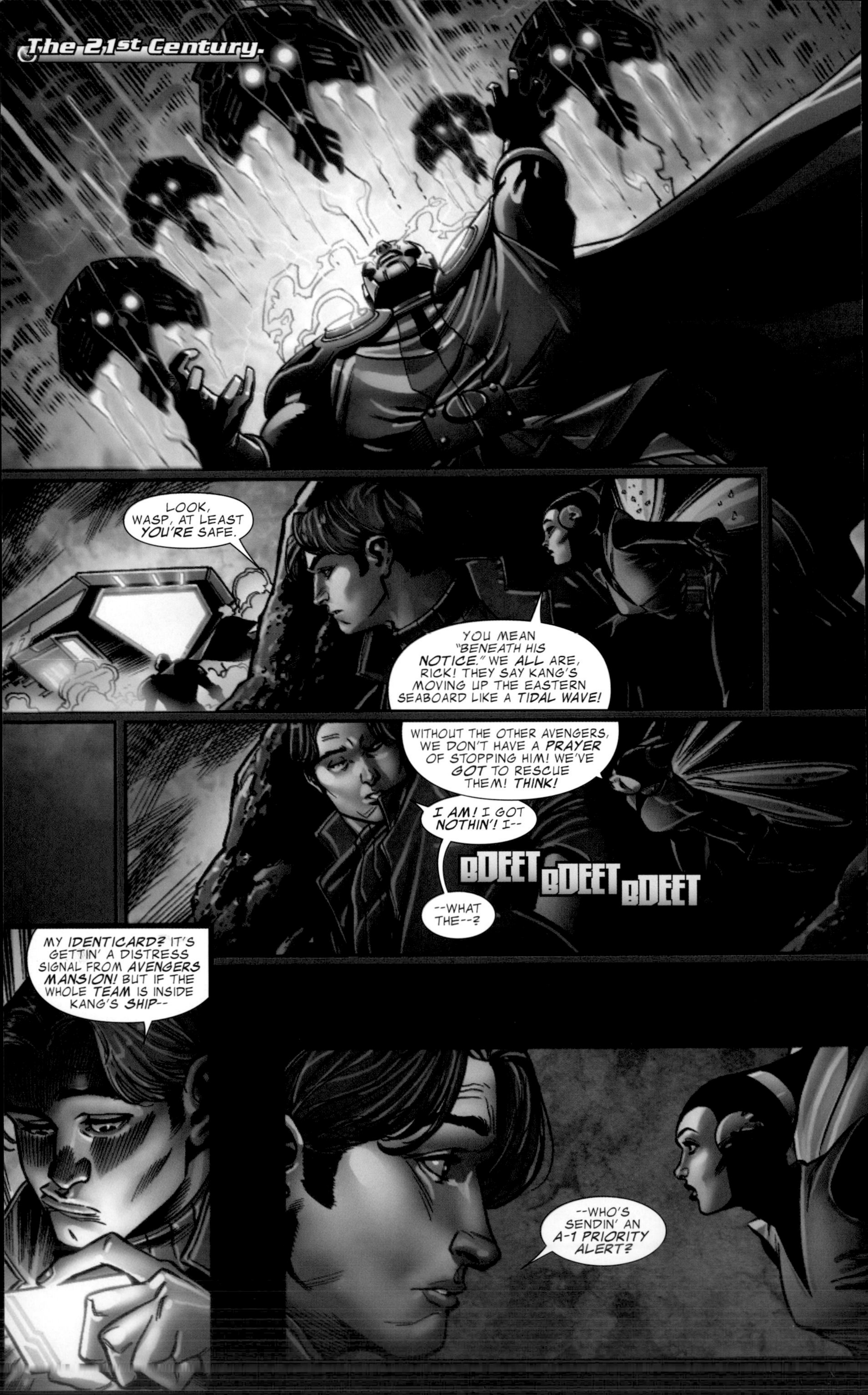
The 21st Century.
LOOK, WASP, AT LEAST YOU'RE SAFE.
YOU MEAN "BENEATH HIS NOTICE." WE ALL ARE, RICK! THEY SAY KANG'S MOVING UP THE EASTERN SEABOARD LIKE A TIDAL WAVE!
WITHOUT THE OTHER AVENGERS, WE DON'T HAVE A PRAYER OF STOPPING HIM! WE'VE GOT TO RESCUE THEM! THINK!
I AM! I GOT NOTHIN'! I--
BDEET BDEET BDEET
--WHAT THE--?
MY IDENTICARD? IT'S GETTIN' A DISTRESS SIGNAL FROM AVENGERS MANSION! BUT IF THE WHOLE TEAM IS INSIDE KANG'S SHIP--
--WHO'S SENDIN' AN A-1 PRIORITY ALERT?

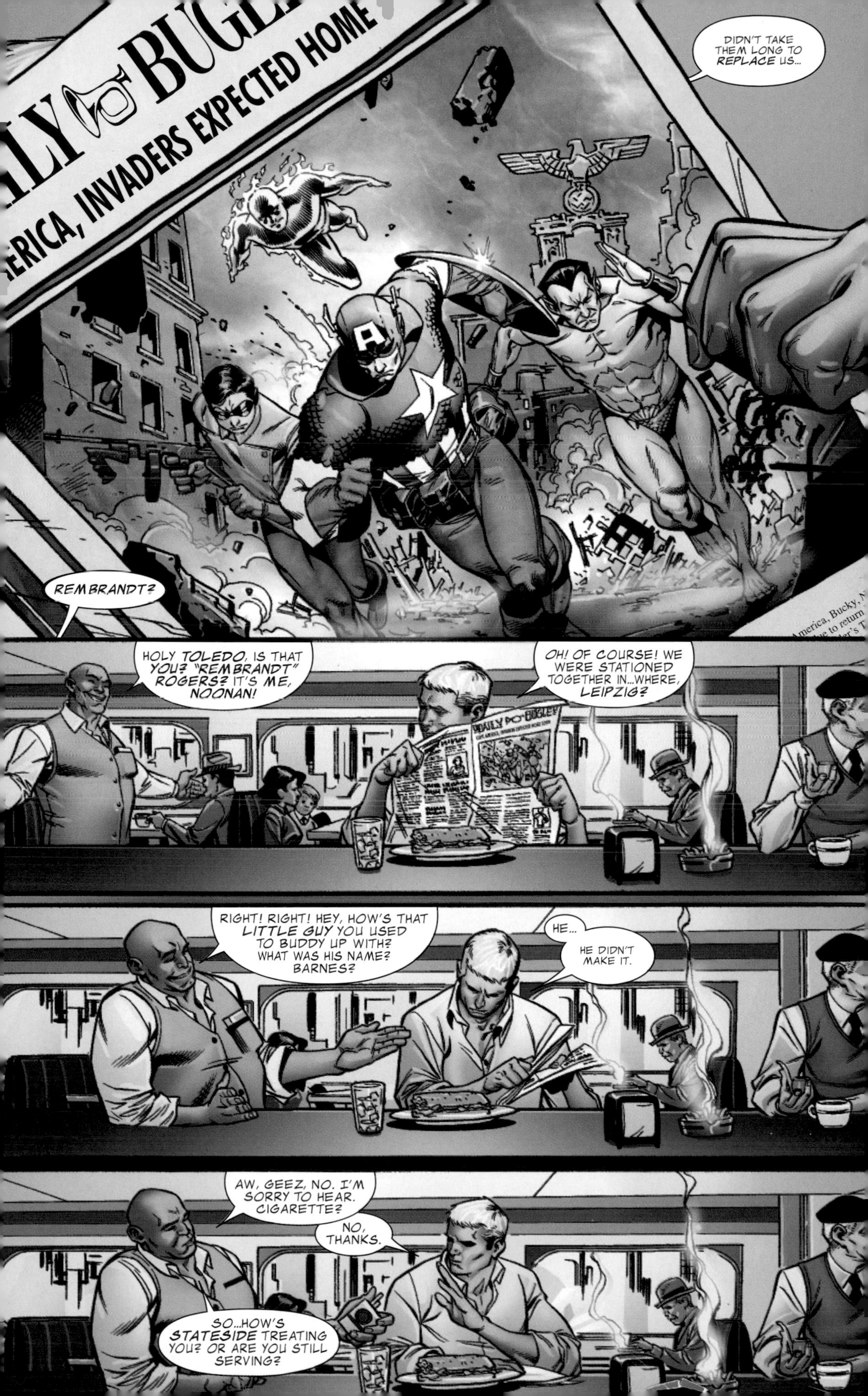
INVADERS EXPECTED HOME
DIDN'T TAKE THEM LONG TO REPLACE US...
REMBRANDT?
HOLY TOLEDO, IS THAT YOU? "REMBRANDT" ROGERS? IT'S ME, NOONAN!
OH! OF COURSE! WE WERE STATIONED TOGETHER IN...WHERE, LEIPZIG?
RIGHT! RIGHT! HEY, HOW'S THAT LITTLE GUY YOU USED TO BUDDY UP WITH? WHAT WAS HIS NAME? BARNES?
HE...
HE DIDN'T MAKE IT.
AW, GEEZ, NO. I'M SORRY TO HEAR. CIGARETTE?
NO, THANKS.
SO...HOW'S STATESIDE TREATING YOU? OR ARE YOU STILL SERVING?

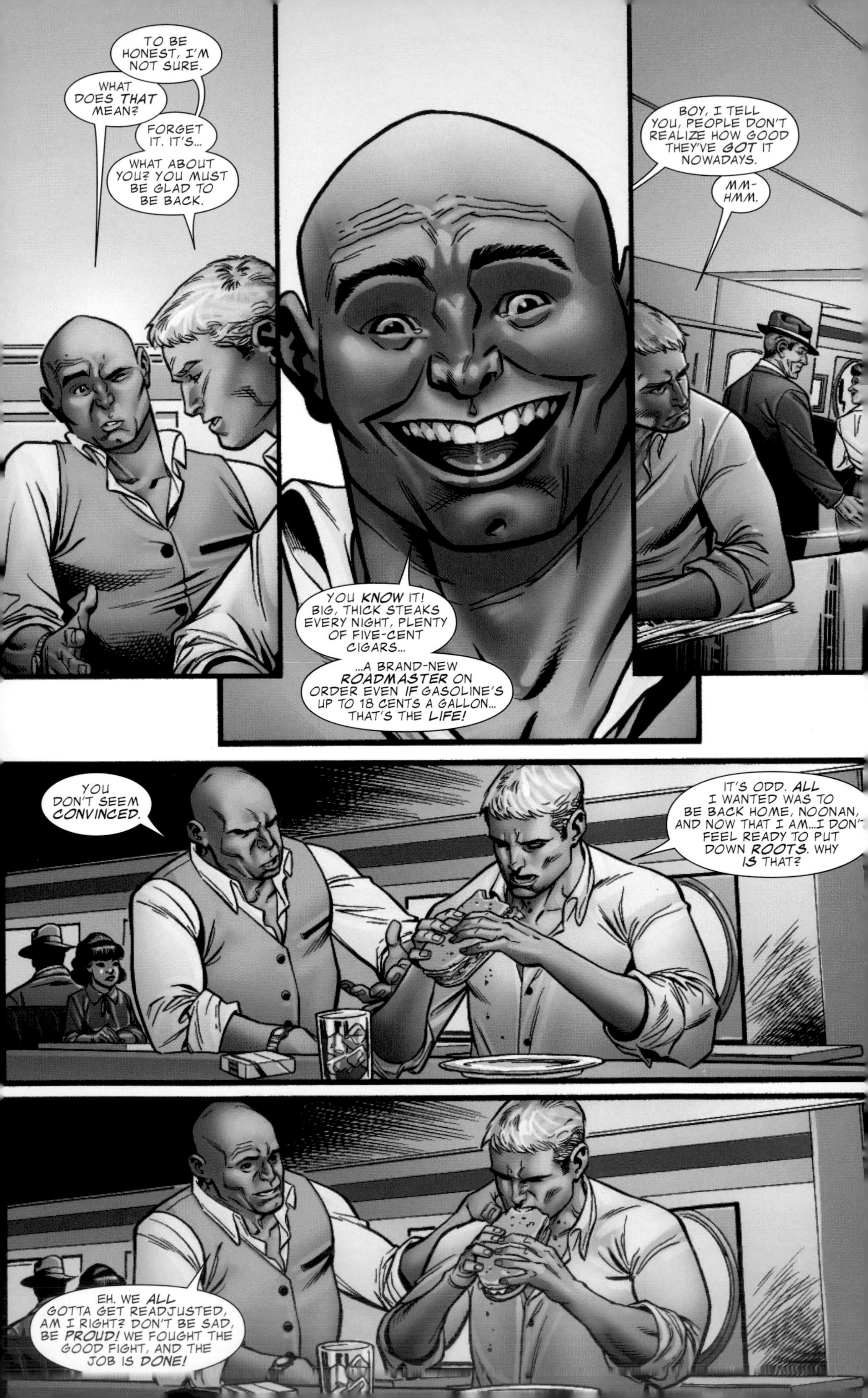
TO BE HONEST, I'M NOT SURE.
WHAT DOES THAT MEAN?
FORGET IT. IT'S...
WHAT ABOUT YOU? YOU MUST BE GLAD TO BE BACK.
YOU KNOW IT! BIG, THICK STEAKS EVERY NIGHT, PLENTY OF FIVE-CENT CIGARS...
...A BRAND-NEW ROADMASTER ON ORDER EVEN IF GASOLINE'S UP TO 18 CENTS A GALLON... THAT'S THE LIFE!
BOY, I TELL YOU, PEOPLE DON'T REALIZE HOW GOOD THEY'VE GOT IT NOWADAYS.
MM-HMM.
YOU DON'T SEEM CONVINCED.
IT'S ODD. ALL I WANTED WAS TO BE BACK HOME, NOONAN, AND NOW THAT I AM...I DON'T FEEL READY TO PUT DOWN ROOTS. WHY IS THAT?
EH. WE ALL GOTTA GET READJUSTED, AM I RIGHT? DON'T BE SAD, BE PROUD! WE FOUGHT THE GOOD FIGHT, AND THE JOB IS DONE!

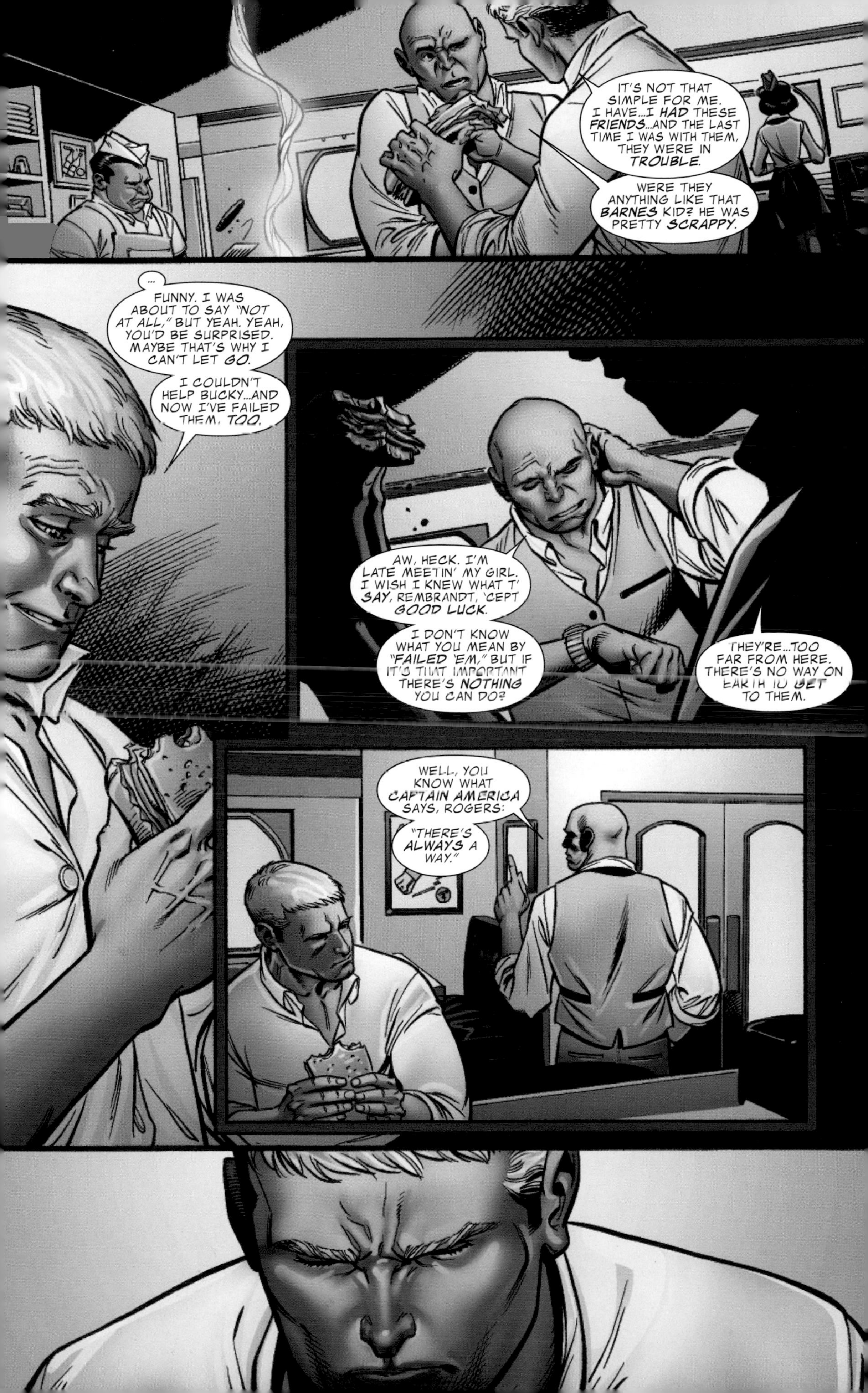
IT'S NOT THAT SIMPLE FOR ME. I HAVE...I HAD THESE FRIENDS...AND THE LAST TIME I WAS WITH THEM, THEY WERE IN TROUBLE.
WERE THEY ANYTHING LIKE THAT BARNES KID? HE WAS PRETTY SCRAPPY.
...
FUNNY. I WAS ABOUT TO SAY "NOT AT ALL," BUT YEAH. YEAH, YOU'D BE SURPRISED. MAYBE THAT'S WHY I CAN'T LET GO.
I COULDN'T HELP BUCKY...AND NOW I'VE FAILED THEM, TOO.
AW, HECK. I'M LATE MEETIN' MY GIRL. I WISH I KNEW WHAT T' SAY, REMBRANDT, 'CEPT GOOD LUCK.
I DON'T KNOW WHAT YOU MEAN BY "FAILED 'EM," BUT IF IT'S THAT IMPORTANT THERE'S NOTHING YOU CAN DO?
THEY'RE...TOO FAR FROM HERE. THERE'S NO WAY ON EARTH TO GET TO THEM.
WELL, YOU KNOW WHAT CAPTAIN AMERICA SAYS, ROGERS:
"THERE'S ALWAYS A WAY."

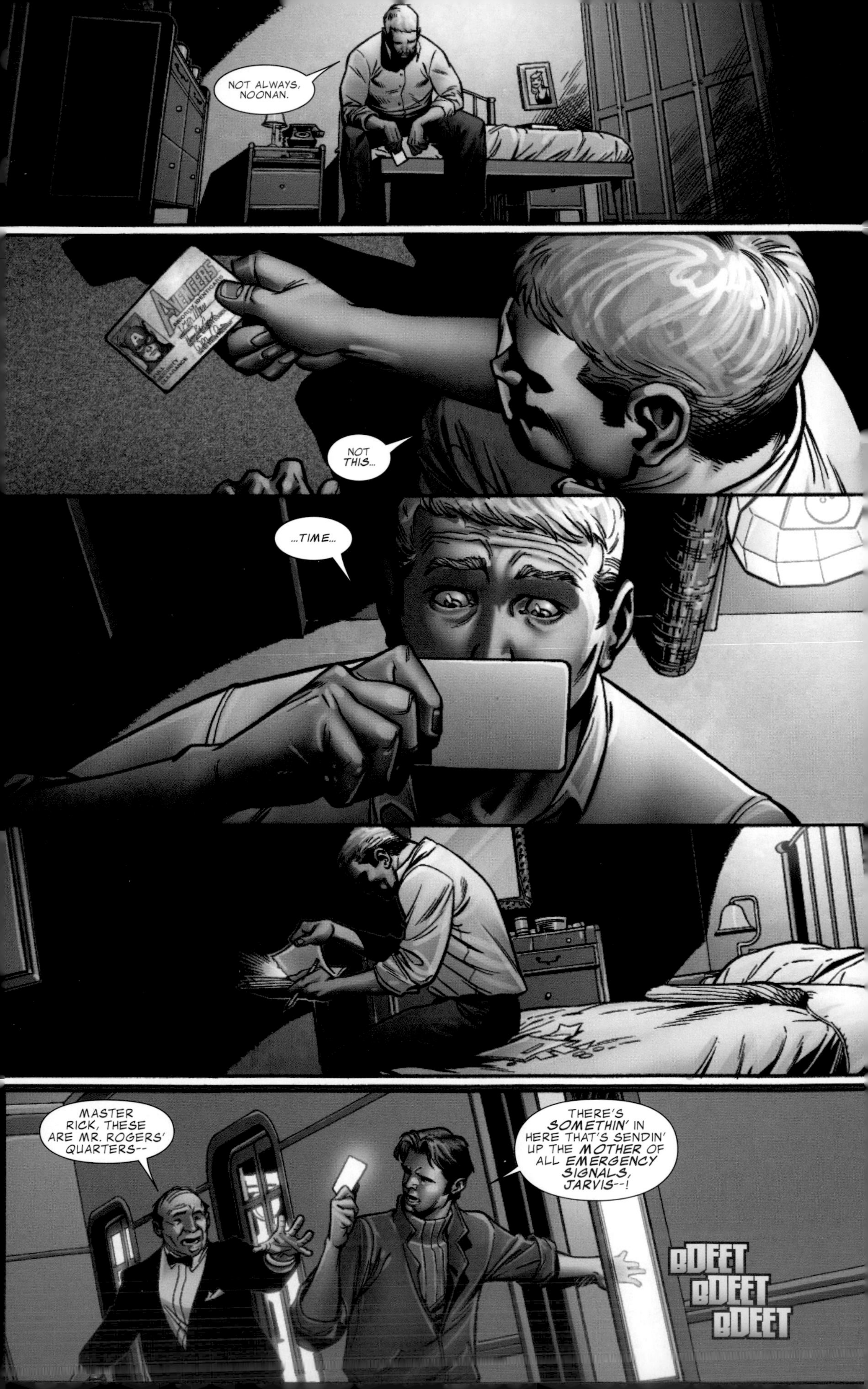
NOT ALWAYS, NOONAN.
NOT THIS...
...TIME...
MASTER RICK, THESE ARE MR. ROGERS' QUARTERS--
THERE'S SOMETHIN' IN HERE THAT'S SENDIN' UP THE MOTHER OF ALL EMERGENCY SIGNALS, JARVIS--!
BDEET BDEET BDEET

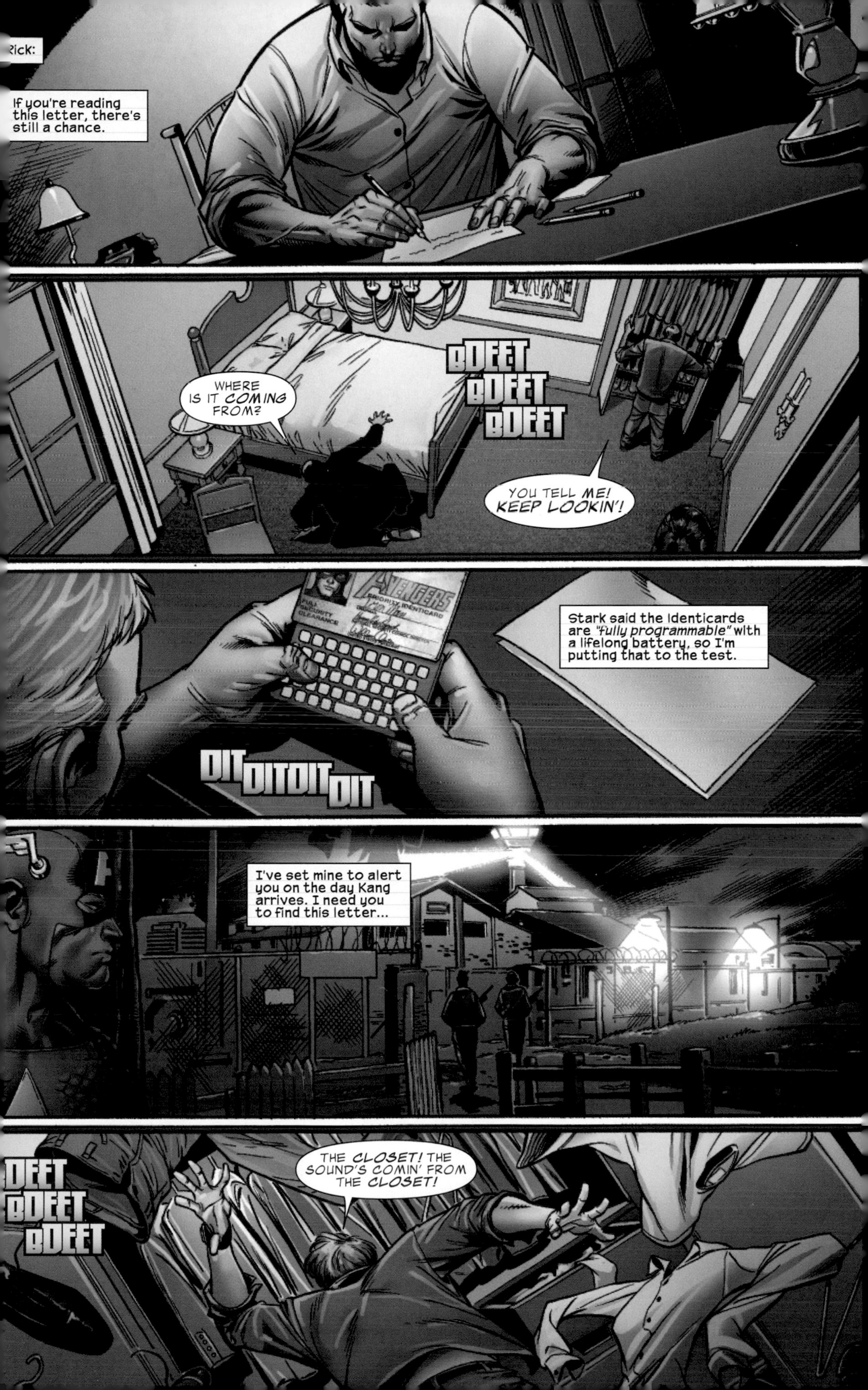
Rick:
If you're reading this letter, there's still a chance.
BDEET BDEET BDEET
WHERE IS IT COMING FROM?
YOU TELL ME! KEEP LOOKIN'!
AVENGERS
FULL SECURITY CLEARANCE
Stark said the Identicards are "fully programmable" with a lifelong battery, so I'm putting that to the test.
DIT DITDIT DIT
I've set mine to alert you on the day Kang arrives. I need you to find this letter...
DEET BDEET BDEET
THE CLOSET! THE SOUND'S COMIN' FROM THE CLOSET!

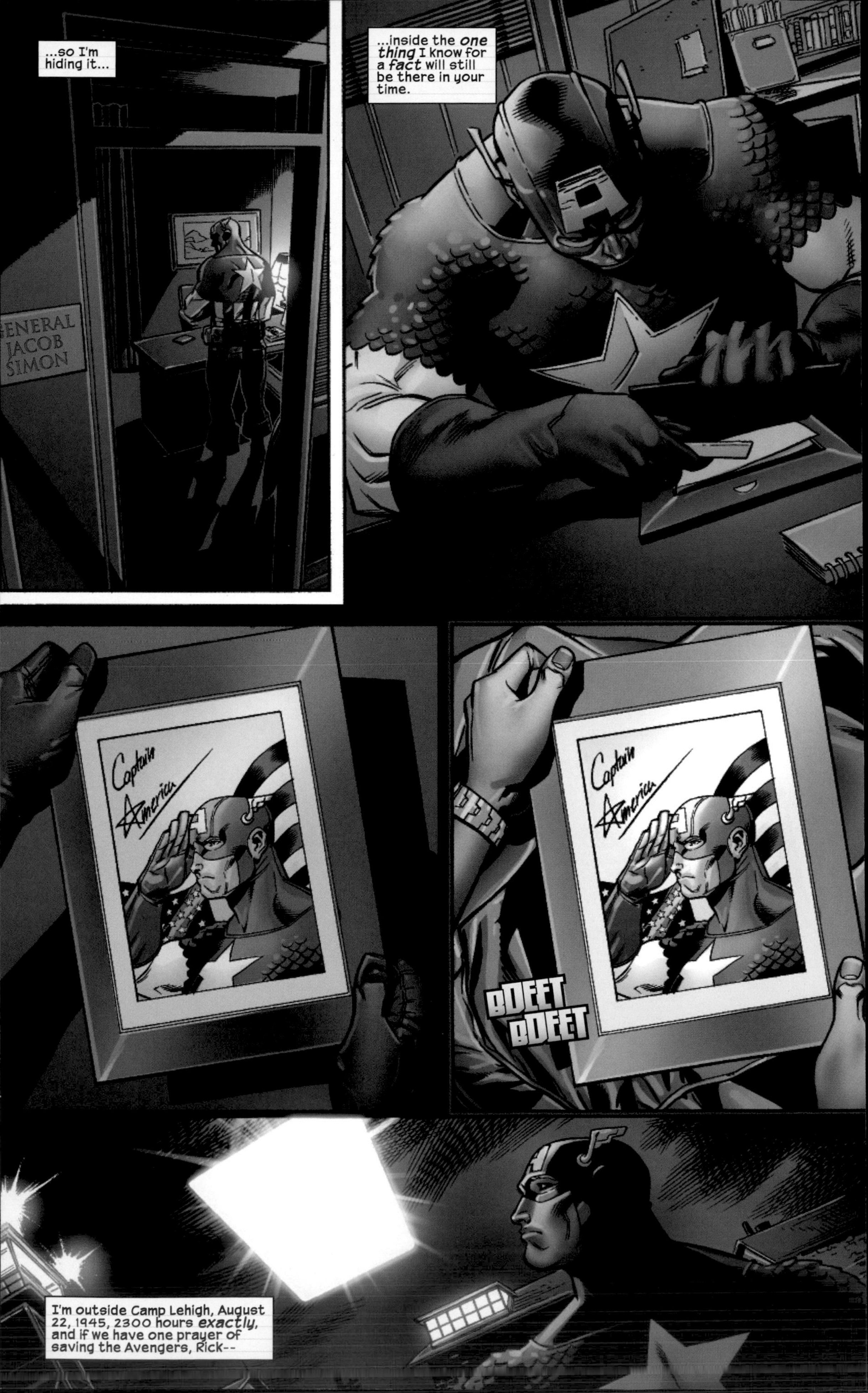
...so I'm hiding it...
GENERAL JACOB SIMON
...inside the one thing I know for a fact will still be there in your time.
Captain America
Captain America
BDEET BDEET
I'm outside Camp Lehigh, August 22, 1945, 2300 hours exactly, and if we have one prayer of saving the Avengers, Rick--

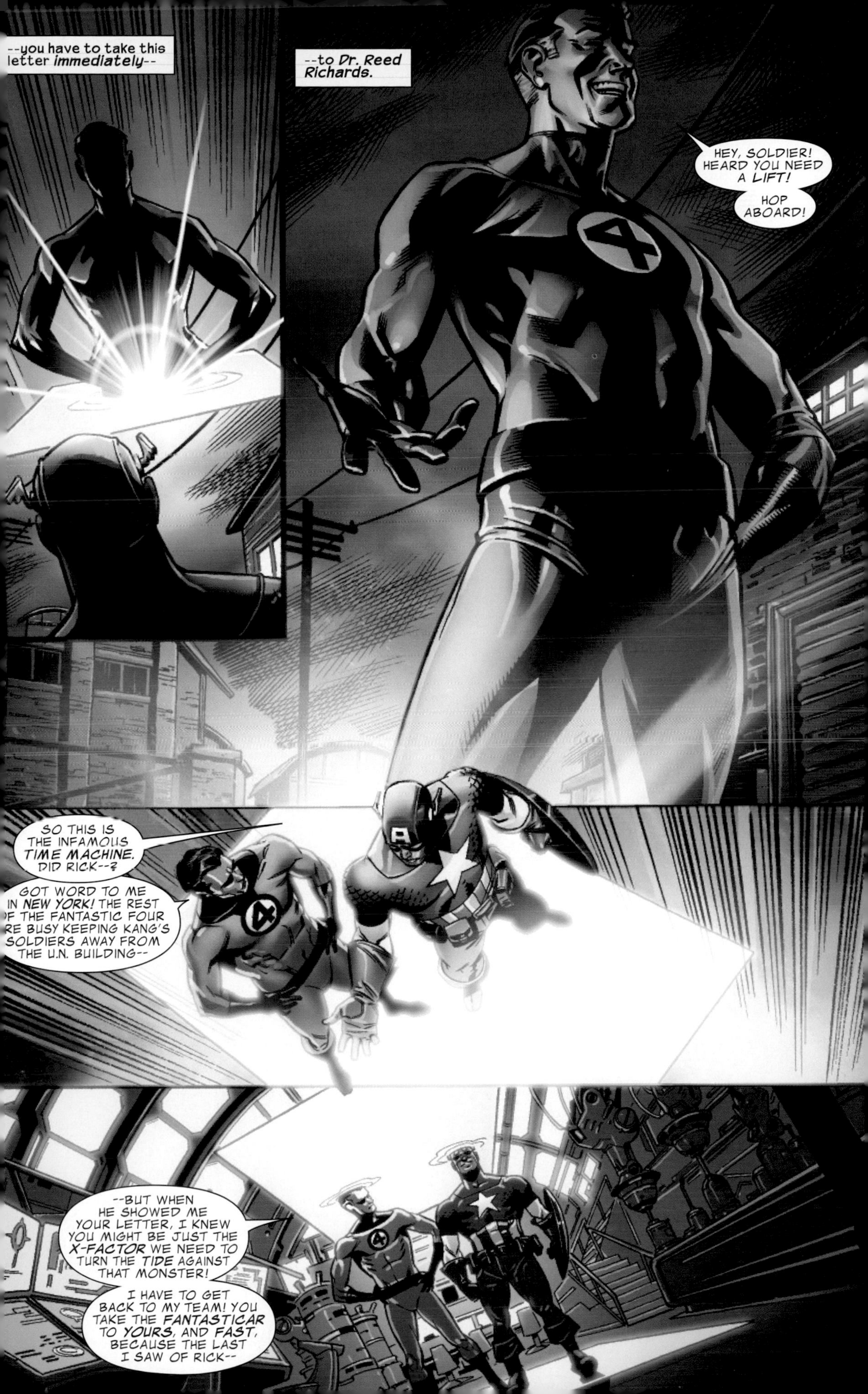
--you have to take this letter *immediately*--
--to *Dr. Reed Richards.*
HEY, SOLDIER! HEARD YOU NEED A *LIFT!*
HOP ABOARD!
SO THIS IS THE INFAMOUS *TIME MACHINE.* DID RICK--?
GOT WORD TO ME IN *NEW YORK!* THE REST OF THE FANTASTIC FOUR ARE BUSY KEEPING KANG'S SOLDIERS AWAY FROM THE U.N. BUILDING--
--BUT WHEN HE SHOWED ME YOUR LETTER, I KNEW YOU MIGHT BE JUST THE *X-FACTOR* WE NEED TO TURN THE *TIDE* AGAINST THAT MONSTER!
I HAVE TO GET BACK TO MY TEAM! YOU TAKE THE *FANTASTICAR* TO *YOURS*, AND *FAST*, BECAUSE THE LAST I SAW OF RICK--

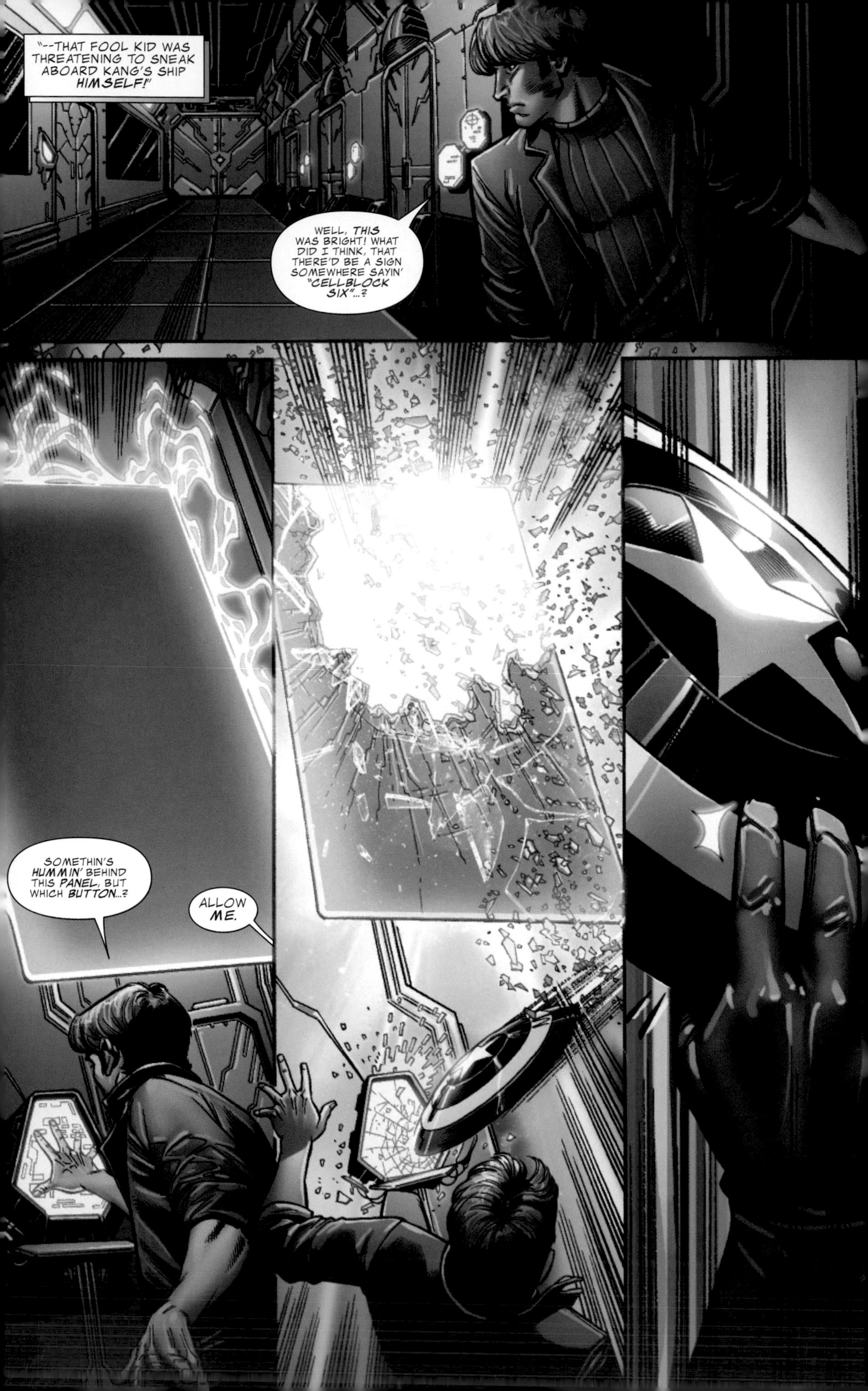
"--THAT FOOL KID WAS THREATENING TO SNEAK ABOARD KANG'S SHIP HIMSELF!"
WELL, THIS WAS BRIGHT! WHAT DID I THINK, THAT THERE'D BE A SIGN SOMEWHERE SAYIN' "CELLBLOCK SIX"...?
SOMETHIN'S HUMMIN' BEHIND THIS PANEL, BUT WHICH BUTTON...?
ALLOW ME.

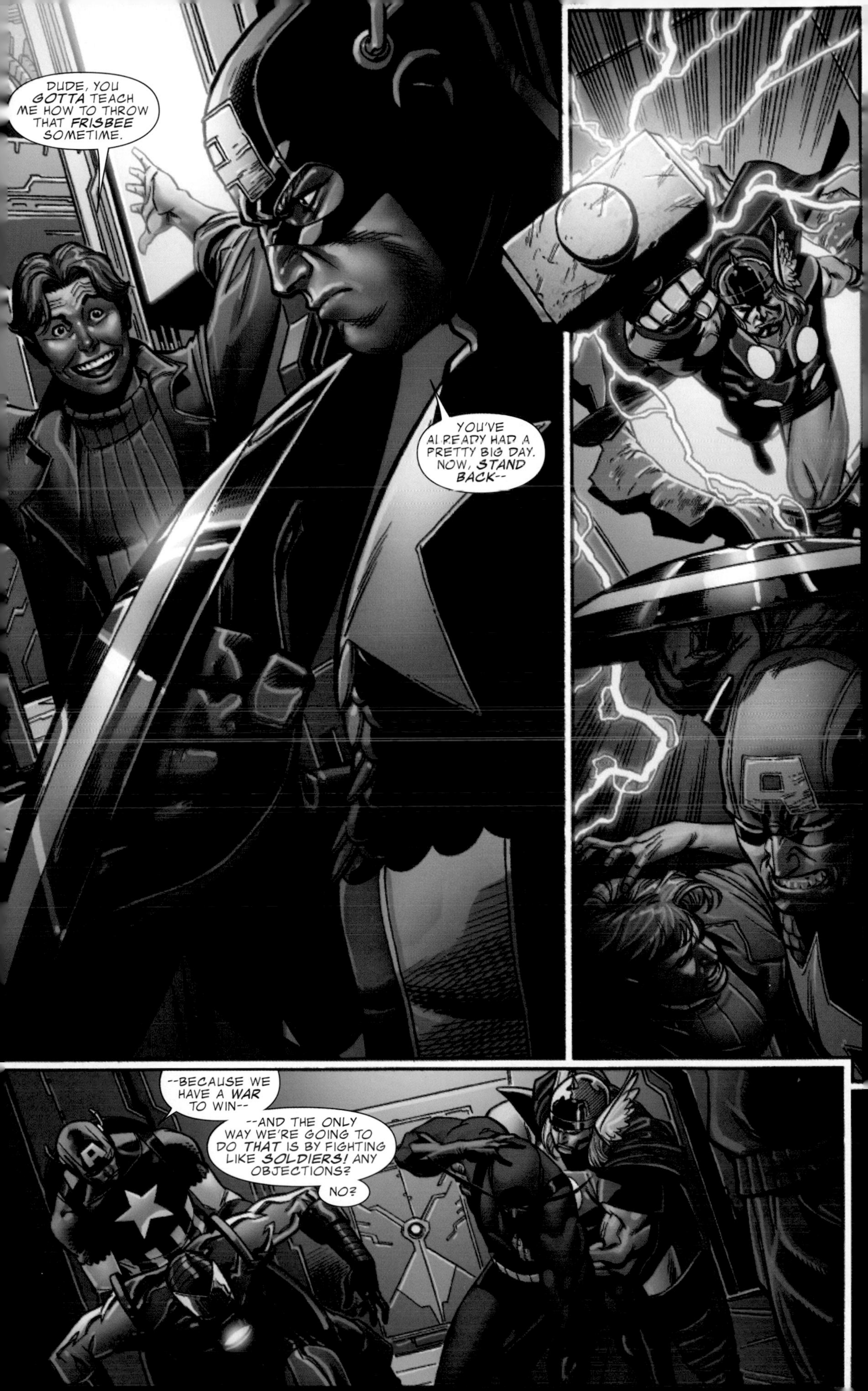
DUDE, YOU GOTTA TEACH ME HOW TO THROW THAT FRISBEE SOMETIME.
YOU'VE ALREADY HAD A PRETTY BIG DAY. NOW, STAND BACK--
--BECAUSE WE HAVE A WAR TO WIN--
--AND THE ONLY WAY WE'RE GOING TO DO THAT IS BY FIGHTING LIKE SOLDIERS! ANY OBJECTIONS?
NO?

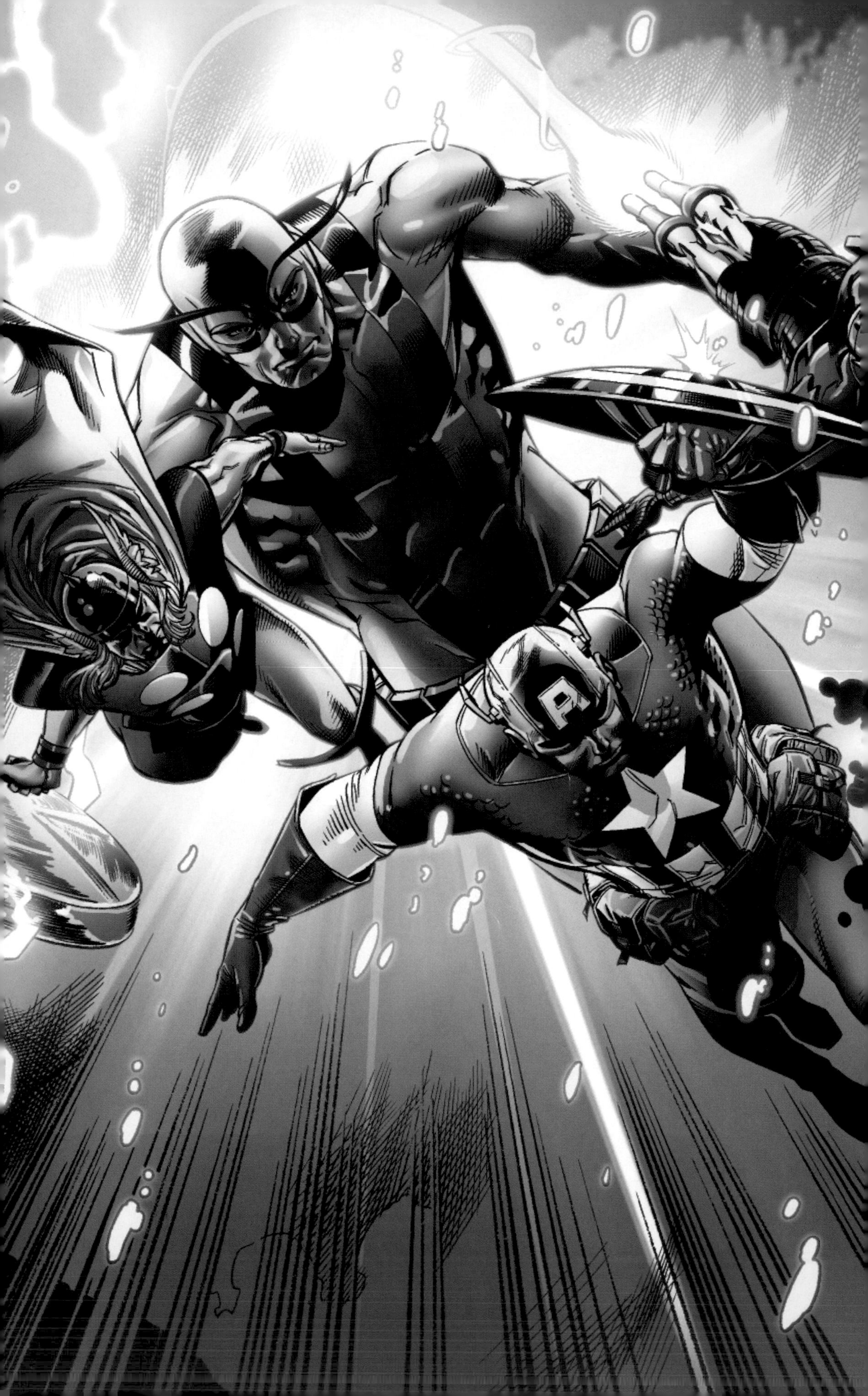

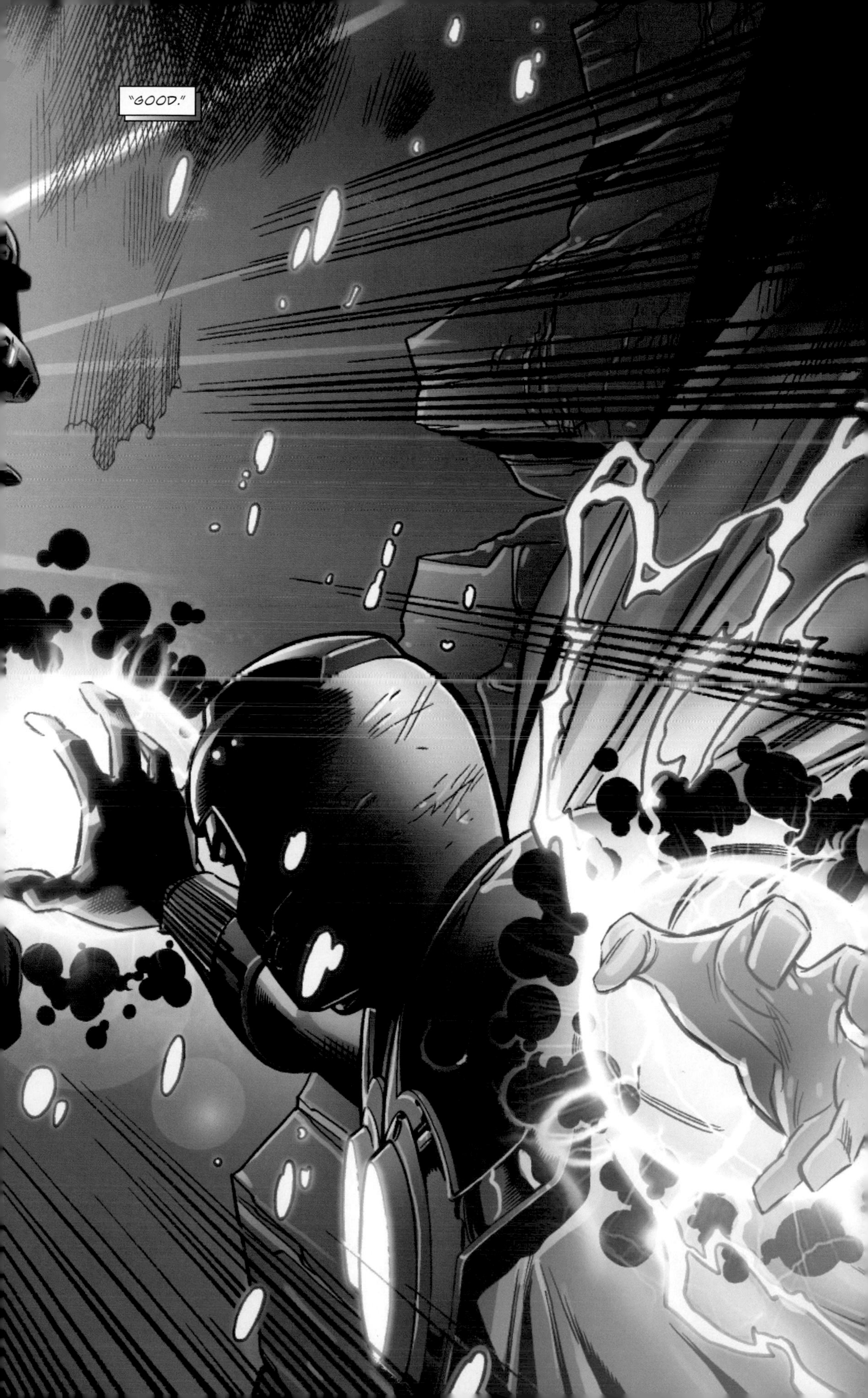
"GOOD."

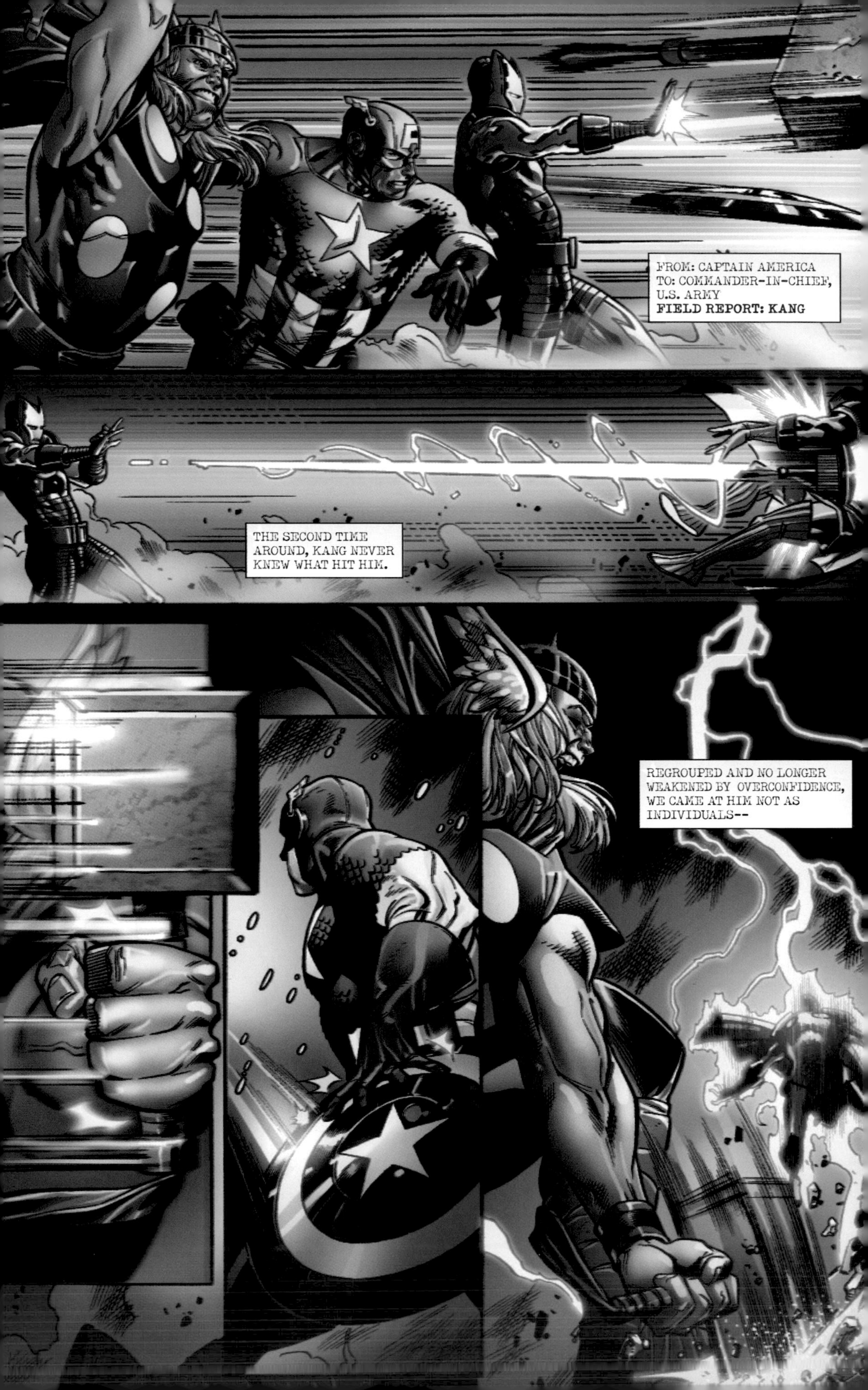
FROM: CAPTAIN AMERICA
TO: COMMANDER-IN-CHIEF,
U.S. ARMY
FIELD REPORT: KANG
THE SECOND TIME AROUND, KANG NEVER KNEW WHAT HIT HIM.
REGROUPED AND NO LONGER WEAKENED BY OVERCONFIDENCE, WE CAME AT HIM NOT AS INDIVIDUALS--

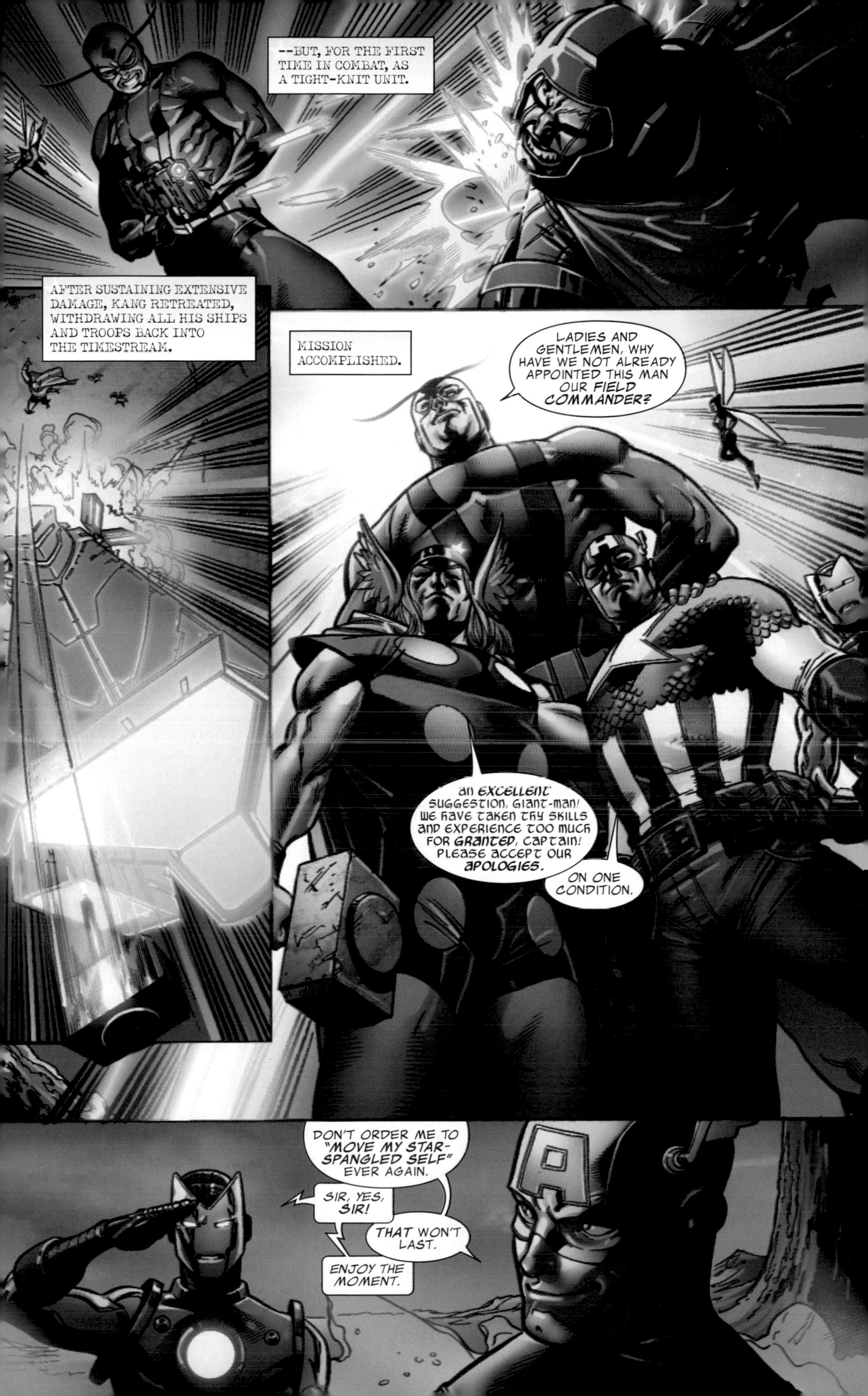
--BUT, FOR THE FIRST TIME IN COMBAT, AS A TIGHT-KNIT UNIT.
AFTER SUSTAINING EXTENSIVE DAMAGE, KANG RETREATED, WITHDRAWING ALL HIS SHIPS AND TROOPS BACK INTO THE TIMESTREAM.
MISSION ACCOMPLISHED.
LADIES AND GENTLEMEN, WHY HAVE WE NOT ALREADY APPOINTED THIS MAN OUR FIELD COMMANDER?
AN EXCELLENT SUGGESTION, GIANT-MAN! WE HAVE TAKEN THY SKILLS AND EXPERIENCE TOO MUCH FOR GRANTED, CAPTAIN! PLEASE ACCEPT OUR APOLOGIES.
ON ONE CONDITION.
DON'T ORDER ME TO "MOVE MY STAR-SPANGLED SELF" EVER AGAIN.
SIR, YES, SIR!
THAT WON'T LAST.
ENJOY THE MOMENT.

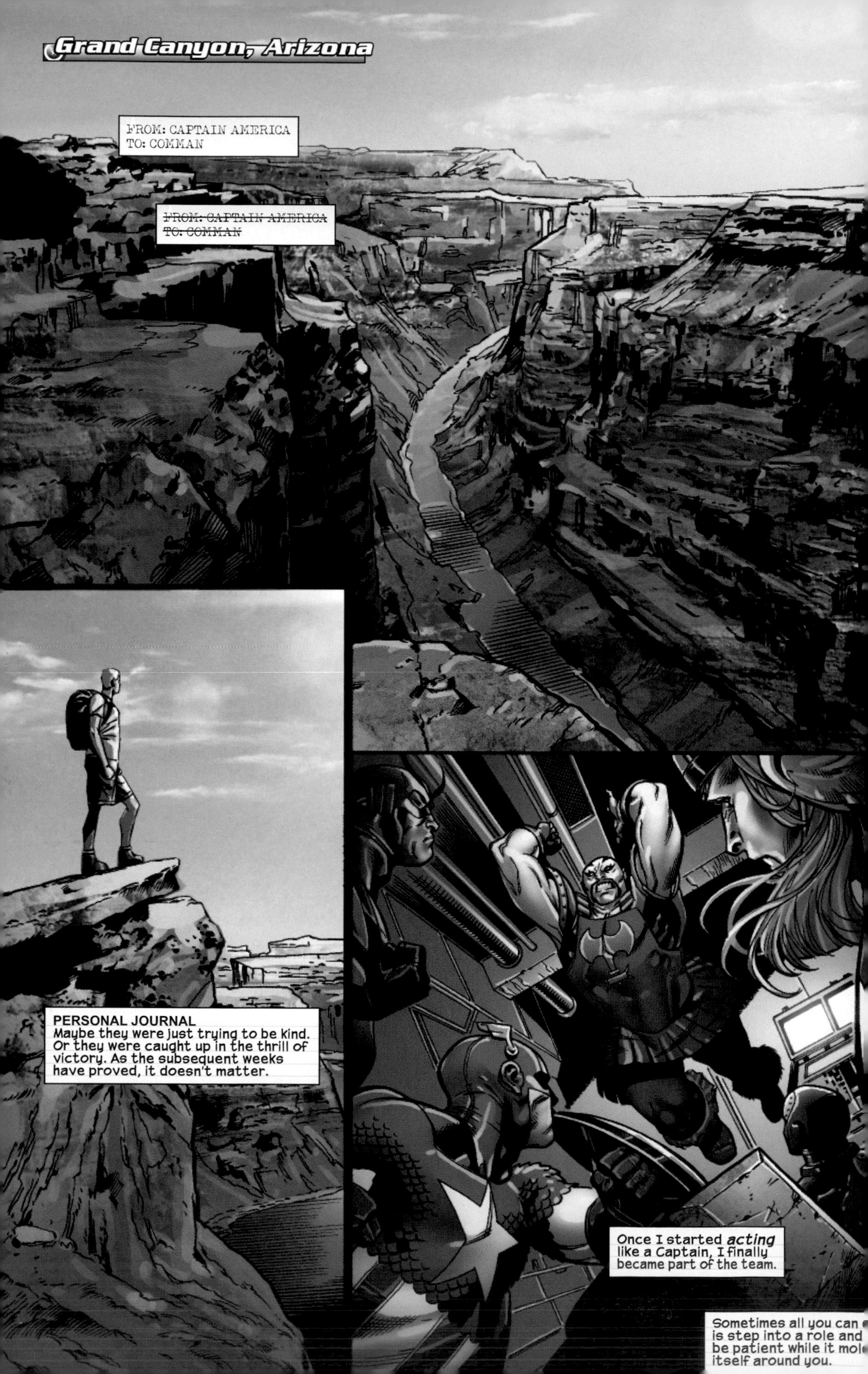

Grand Canyon, Arizona
FROM: CAPTAIN AMERICA
TO: COMMAN
~~FROM: CAPTAIN AMERICA~~
~~TO: COMMAN~~
PERSONAL JOURNAL
Maybe they were just trying to be kind. Or they were caught up in the thrill of victory. As the subsequent weeks have proved, it doesn't matter.
Once I started *acting* like a Captain, I finally became part of the team.
Sometimes all you can
is step into a role and
be patient while it mol
itself around you.

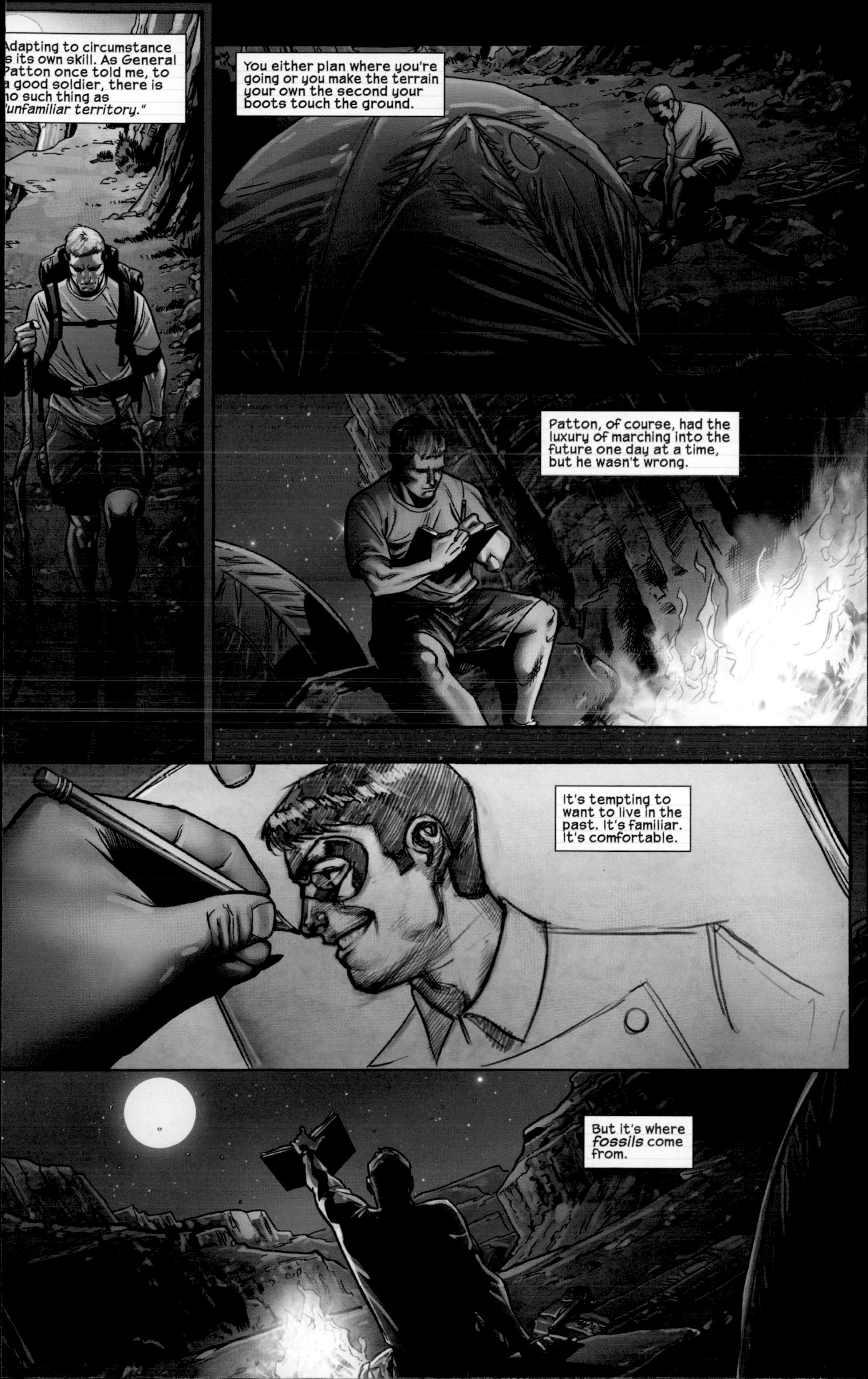
Adapting to circumstance is its own skill. As General Patton once told me, to a good soldier, there is no such thing as "unfamiliar territory."
You either plan where you're going or you make the terrain your own the second your boots touch the ground.
Patton, of course, had the luxury of marching into the future one day at a time, but he wasn't wrong.
It's tempting to want to live in the past. It's familiar. It's comfortable.
But it's where *fossils* come from.

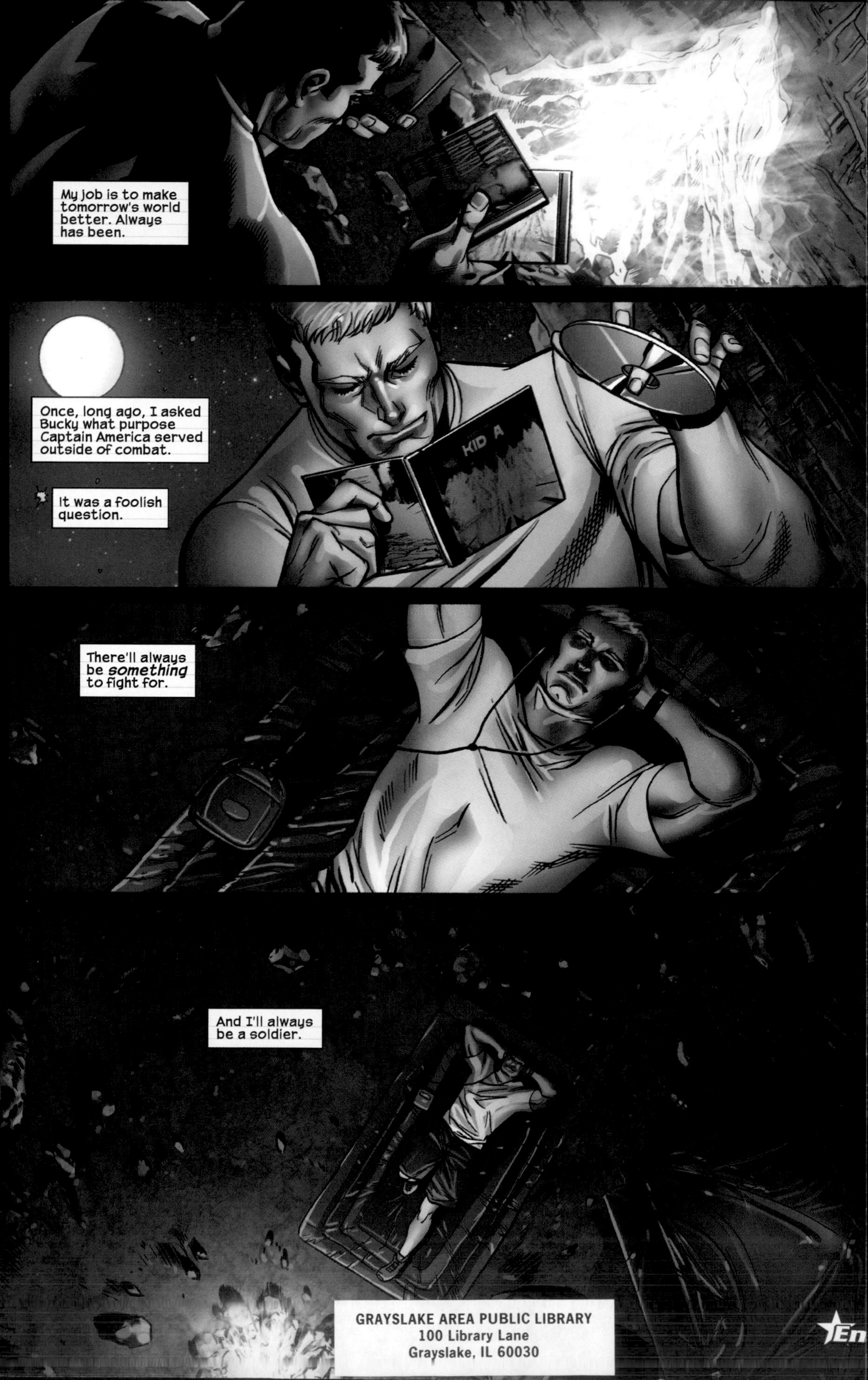
My job is to make tomorrow's world better. Always has been.
KID A
Once, long ago, I asked Bucky what purpose Captain America served outside of combat.
It was a foolish question.
There'll always be *something* to fight for.
And I'll always be a soldier.
End